SHOWDOWN ON THE SMUGGLER'S MOON: VOLUME 3

It is a period of renewed hope for the Rebellion. The evil Galactic Empire's greatest weapon, the Death Star, has been destroyed by the young rebel pilot Luke Skywalker.

But Skywalker's quest to learn the ways of the Jedi continues. That quest has brought him to the notorious Smuggler's Moon of Nar Shaddaa, where his lightsaber has made him a target for a particularly crafty pickpocket.

Meanwhile, Princess Leia and Han Solo have encountered some surprises of their own. While searching the galaxy for a suitable site for the new rebel base, they ran afoul of Imperial patrol ships. Now hiding out on a remote planet, they find themselves facing a far more shocking encounter.

Her name is Sana Solo. She claims to be Han Solo's wife.

And she seems very interested in collecting the bounty on the rebel princess's head....

JASON AARON
Writer

STUART IMMONEN
Artist

WADE VON GRAWBADGER
Inker

JUSTIN PONSOR
Colorist

CHRIS ELIOPOULOS
Letterer

IMMONEN, VON GRAWBADGER, PONSOR
Cover Artists

HEATHER ANTOS
Assistant Editor

JORDAN D. WHITE
Editor

C.B. CEBULSKI
Executive Editor

AXEL ALONSO
Editor In Chief

JOE QUESADA
Chief Creative Officer

DAN BUCKLEY
Publisher

For Lucasfilm:
Creative Director MICHAEL SIGLAIN
Senior Editor FRANK PARISI
Lucasfilm Story Group RAYNE ROBERTS, PABLO HIDALGO, LELAND CHEE

DISNEY | LUCASFILM

ABDO
Spotlight

ABDOPUBLISHING.COM

Reinforced library bound edition published in 2017 by Spotlight,
a division of ABDO, PO Box 398166, Minneapolis, Minnesota 55439.
Spotlight produces high-quality reinforced library bound editions for
schools and libraries. Published by agreement with Marvel Characters, Inc.

Printed in the United States of America, North Mankato, Minnesota.
092016
012017

THIS BOOK CONTAINS
RECYCLED MATERIALS

marvelkids.com

PUBLISHER'S CATALOGING IN PUBLICATION DATA

Names: Aaron, Jason, author. | Bianchi, Simone ; Ponsor, Justin ; Immonen, Stuart ; Von Grawbadger, Wade, illustrators.
Title: Showdown on the Smuggler's Moon / writer: Jason Aaron ; art: Simone Bianchi ; Justin Ponsor ; Stuart Immomen ; Wade Von Grawbadger.
Description: Reinforced library bound edition. | Minneapolis, Minnesota : Spotlight, 2017. | Series: Star Wars : Showdown on the Smuggler's Moon
Summary: After reading Ben Kenobi's journal, Luke Skywalker is imprisoned during his search for a Jedi Temple, while Han and Leia flee from some Imperial troops with help from an unexpected foe, and Chewbacca and C-3PO are attacked by a mysterious bounty hunter.
Identifiers: LCCN 2016941802 | ISBN 9781614795544 (volume 1) | ISBN 9781614795551 (volume 2) | ISBN 9781614795568 (volume 3) | ISBN 9781614795575 (volume 4) | ISBN 9781614795582 (volume 5) | ISBN 9781614795599 (volume 6)
Subjects: LCSH: Star Wars fiction--Comic books, strips, etc.--Juvenile fiction. | Graphic novels--Juvenile fiction.
Classification: DDC 741.5--dc23
LC record available at https://lccn.loc.gov/2016941802

ABDO
Spotlight

A Division of ABDO
abdopublishing.com

STAR WARS™

SHOWDOWN ON THE SMUGGLER'S MOON

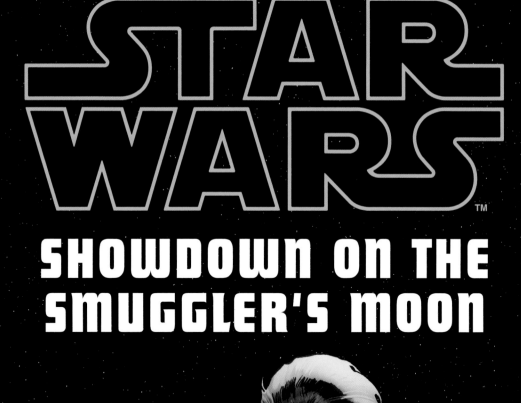

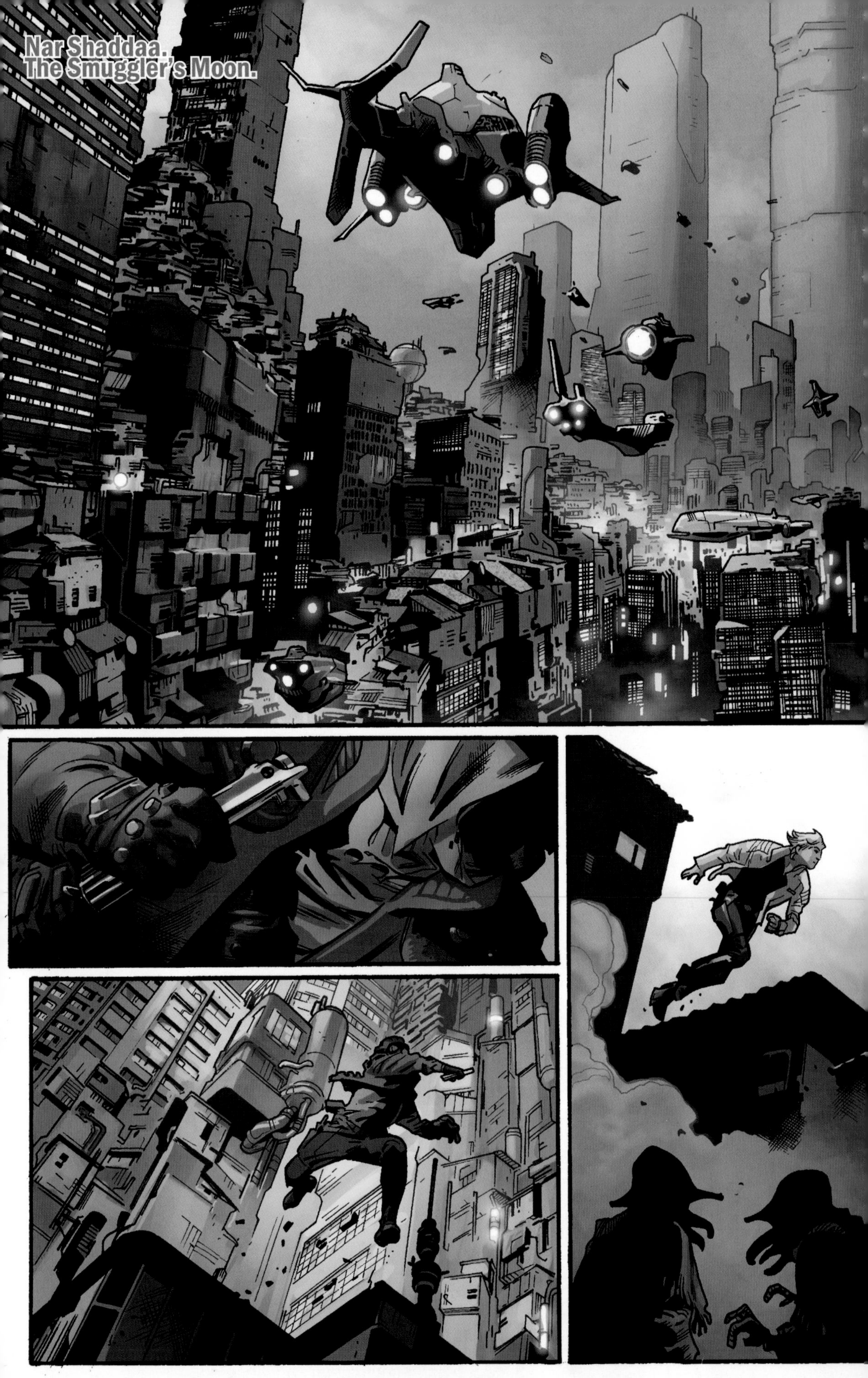
Nar Shaddaa.
The Smuggler's Moon.

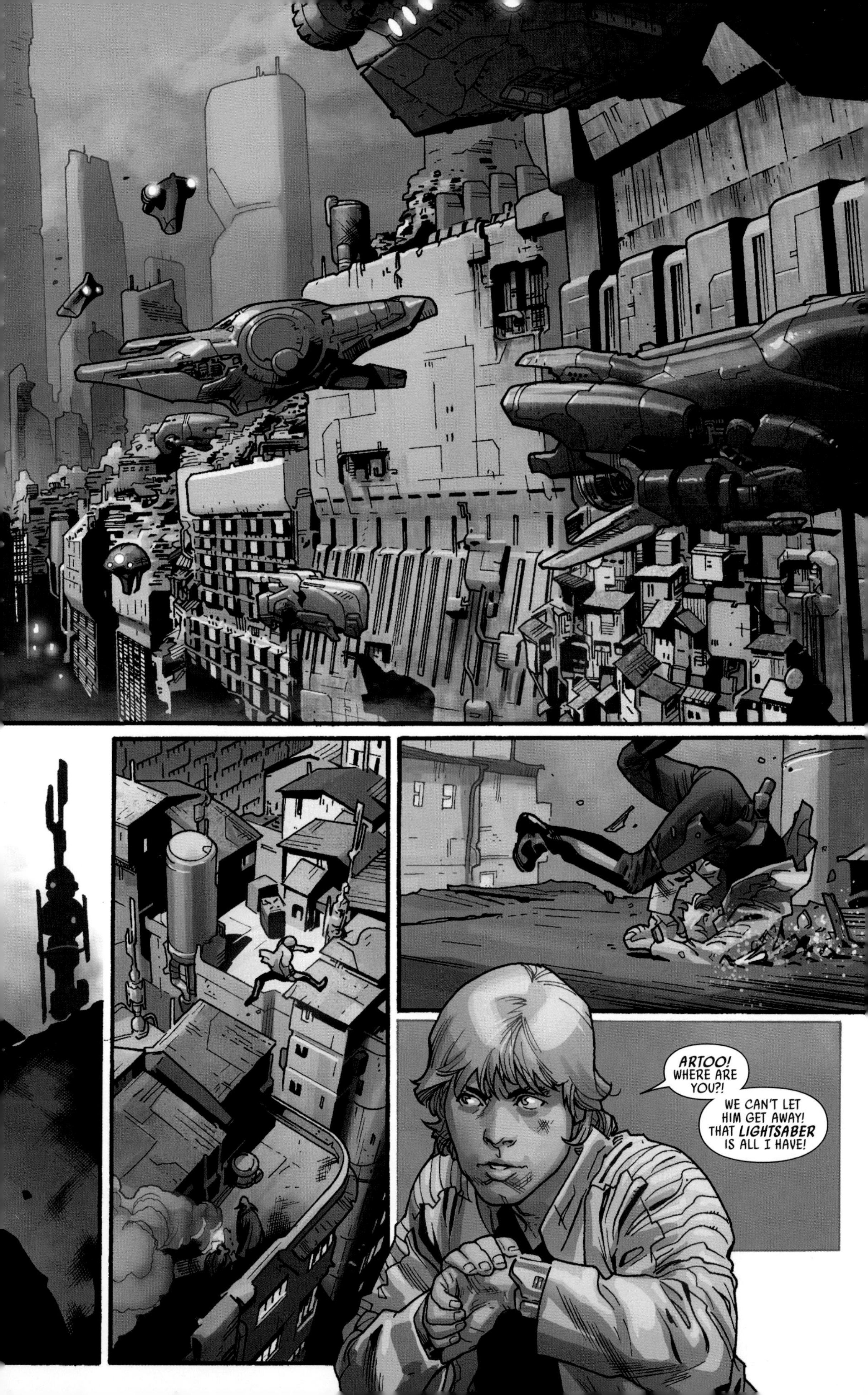
ARTOO! WHERE ARE YOU?!
WE CAN'T LET HIM GET AWAY! THAT LIGHTSABER IS ALL I HAVE!

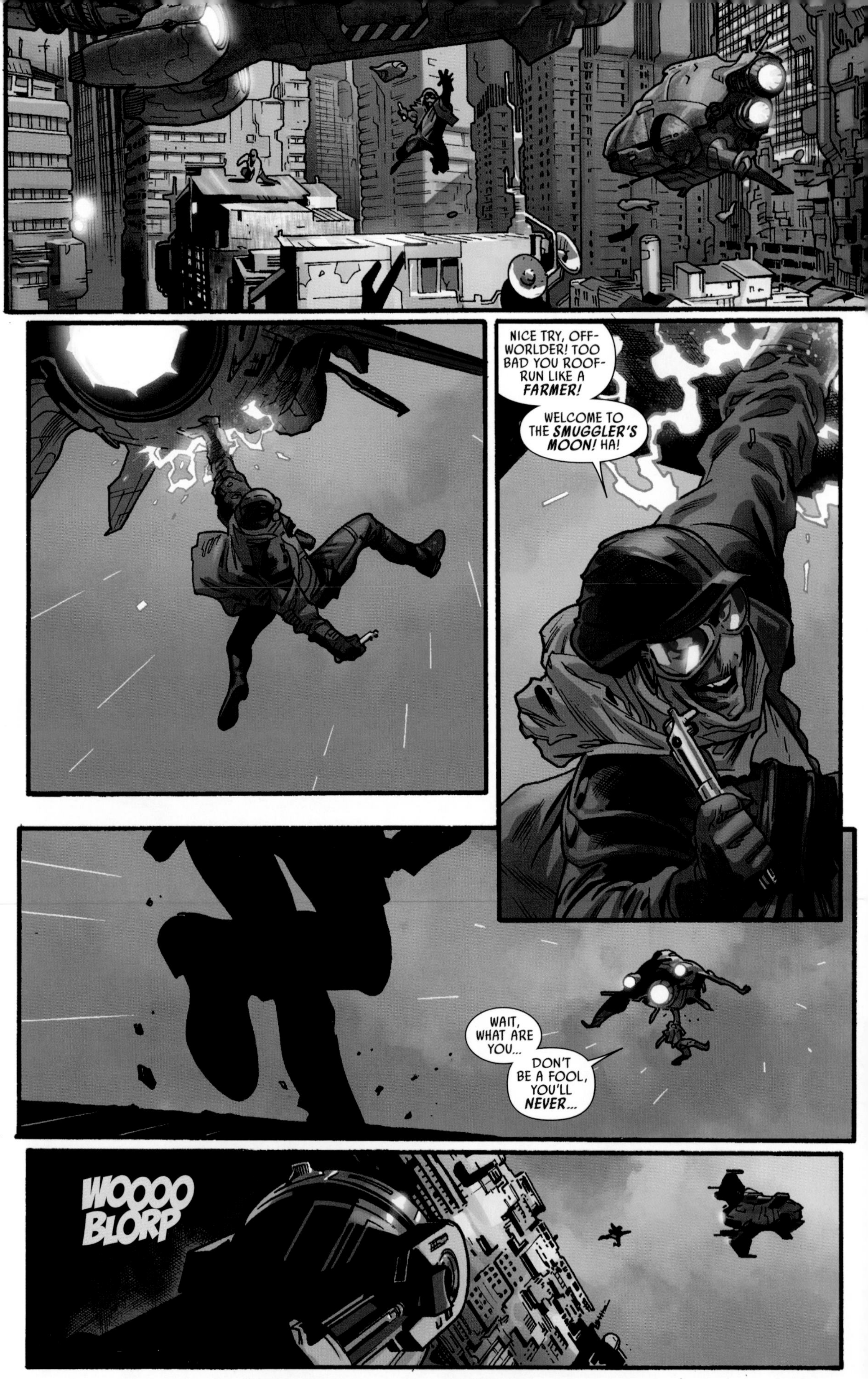

NICE TRY, OFF-WORLDER! TOO BAD YOU ROOF-RUN LIKE A FARMER!
WELCOME TO THE SMUGGLER'S MOON! HA!
WAIT, WHAT ARE YOU...
DON'T BE A FOOL, YOU'LL NEVER...
WOOOO BLORP

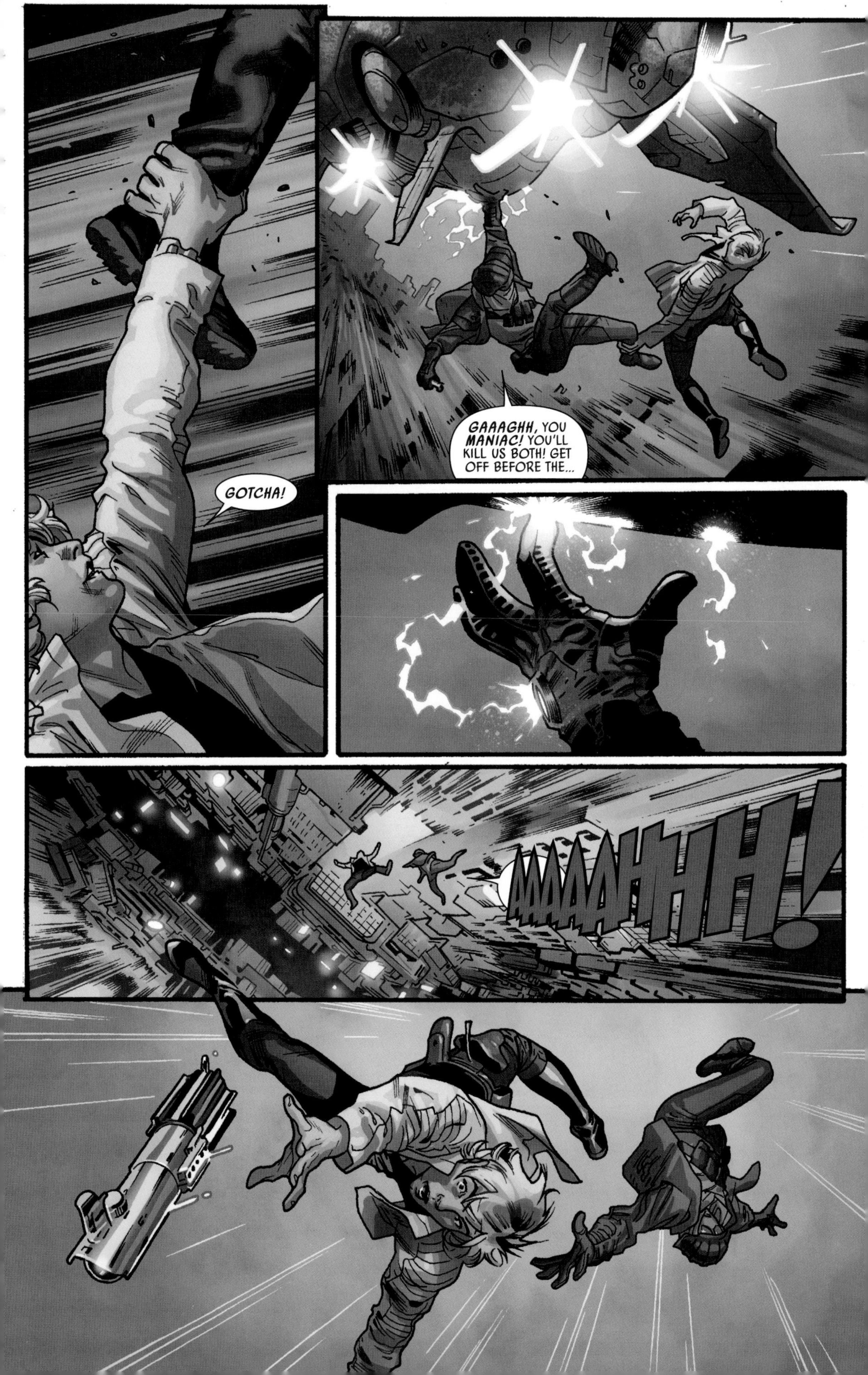
GAAAGHH, YOU MANIAC! YOU'LL KILL US BOTH! GET OFF BEFORE THE...
GOTCHA!
AAAAAHHH!

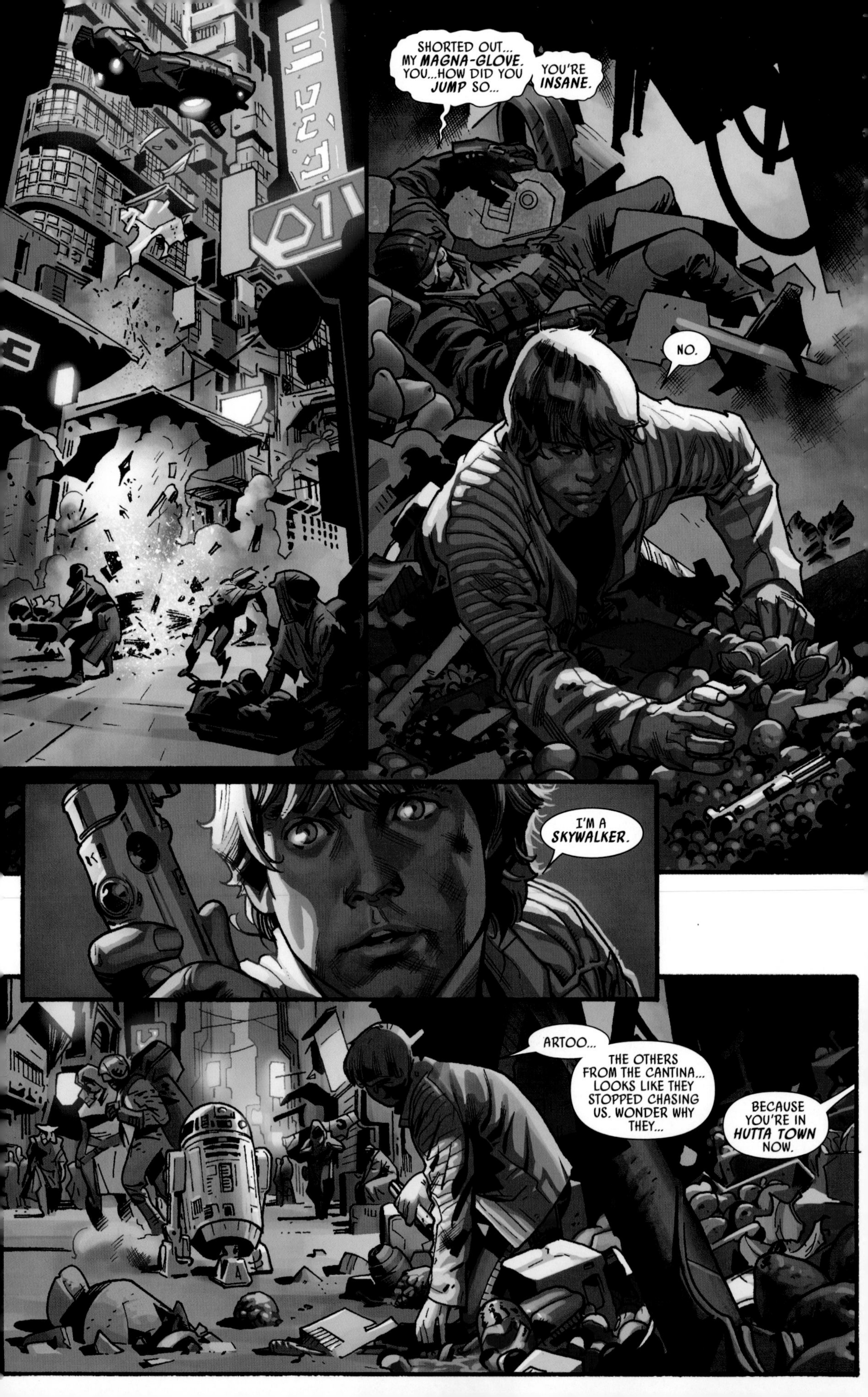
SHORTED OUT... MY MAGNA-GLOVE. YOU...HOW DID YOU JUMP SO...
YOU'RE INSANE.
NO.
I'M A SKYWALKER.
ARTOO...
THE OTHERS FROM THE CANTINA... LOOKS LIKE THEY STOPPED CHASING US. WONDER WHY THEY...
BECAUSE YOU'RE IN HUTTA TOWN NOW.

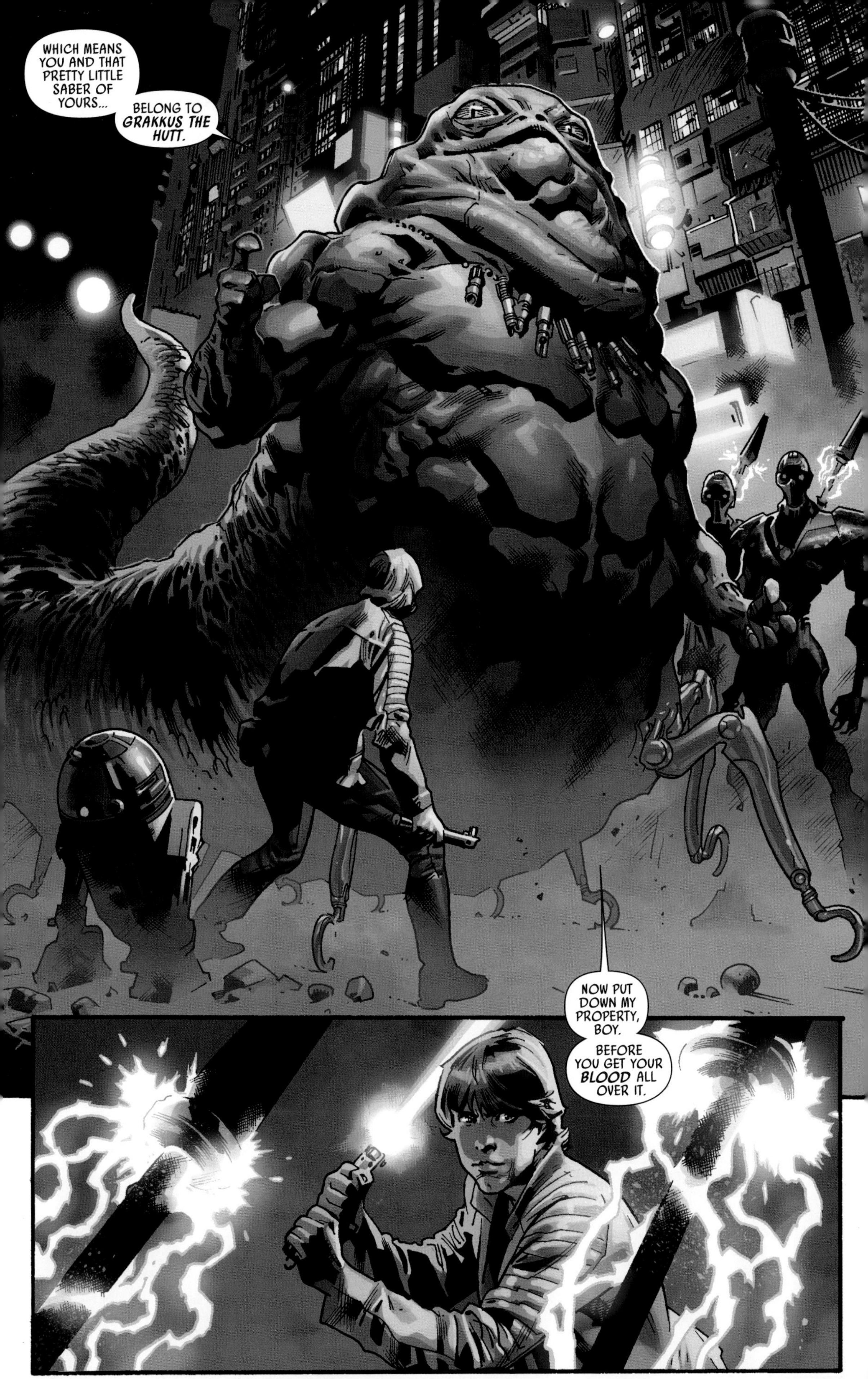
WHICH MEANS YOU AND THAT PRETTY LITTLE SABER OF YOURS...
BELONG TO GRAKKUS THE HUTT.
NOW PUT DOWN MY PROPERTY, BOY.
BEFORE YOU GET YOUR BLOOD ALL OVER IT.

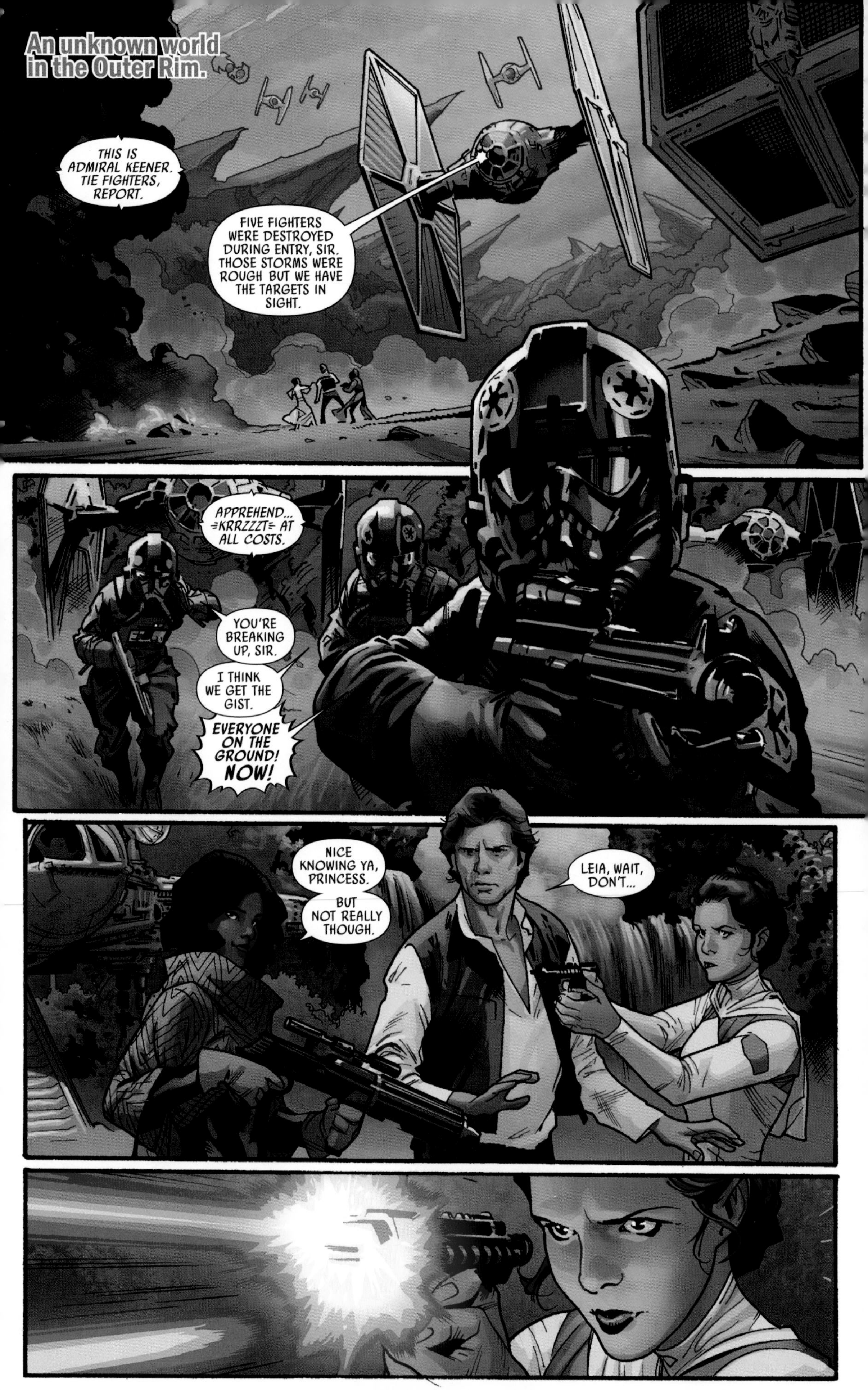
An unknown world in the Outer Rim.
THIS IS ADMIRAL KEENER. TIE FIGHTERS, REPORT.
FIVE FIGHTERS WERE DESTROYED DURING ENTRY, SIR. THOSE STORMS WERE ROUGH BUT WE HAVE THE TARGETS IN SIGHT.
APPREHEND... =KRRZZZT= AT ALL COSTS.
YOU'RE BREAKING UP, SIR.
I THINK WE GET THE GIST.
EVERYONE ON THE GROUND! NOW!
NICE KNOWING YA, PRINCESS.
BUT NOT REALLY THOUGH.
LEIA, WAIT, DON'T...

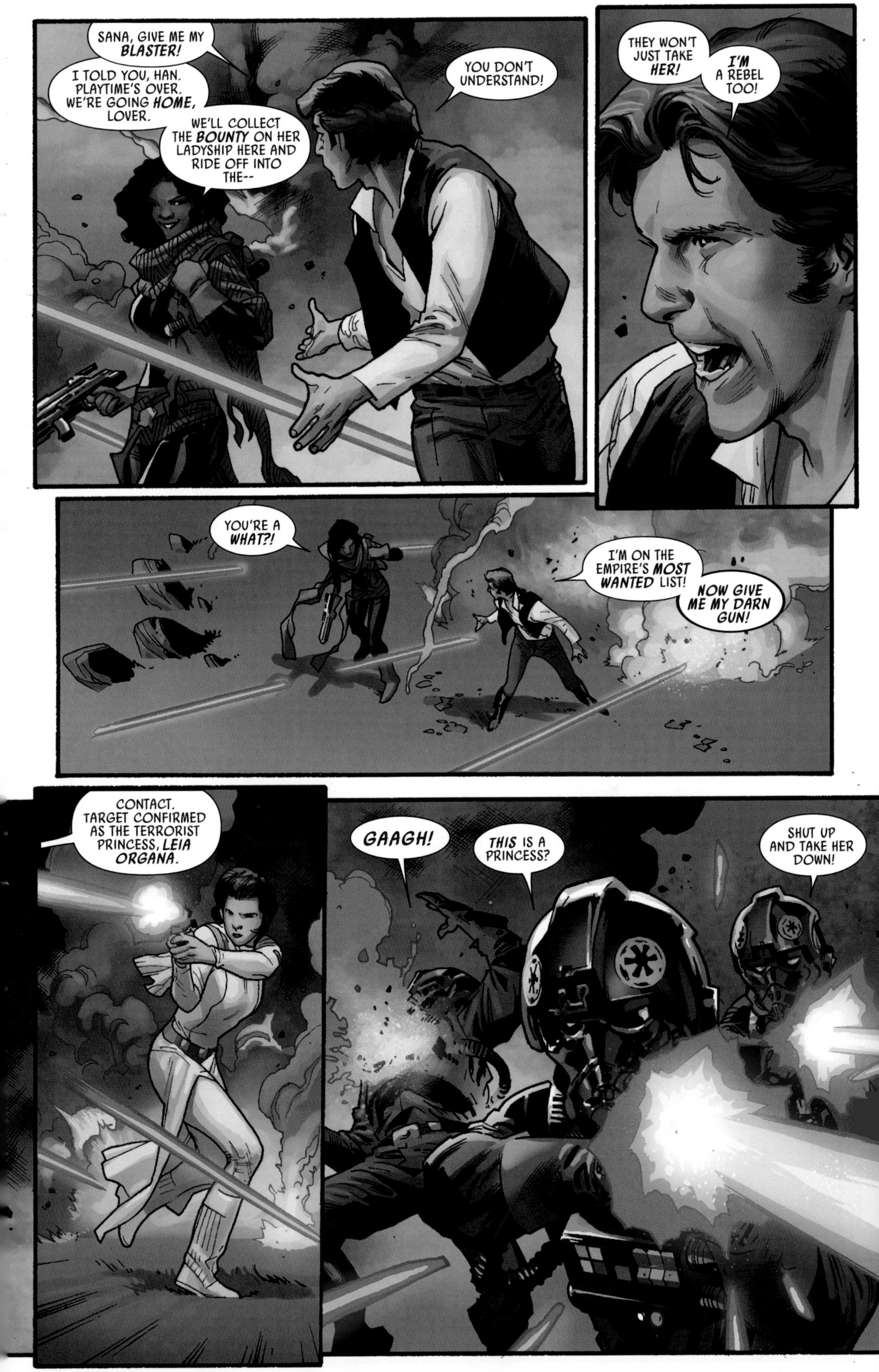
SANA, GIVE ME MY BLASTER!
I TOLD YOU, HAN. PLAYTIME'S OVER. WE'RE GOING HOME, LOVER.
WE'LL COLLECT THE BOUNTY ON HER LADYSHIP HERE AND RIDE OFF INTO THE--
YOU DON'T UNDERSTAND!
THEY WON'T JUST TAKE HER!
I'M A REBEL TOO!
YOU'RE A WHAT?!
I'M ON THE EMPIRE'S MOST WANTED LIST!
NOW GIVE ME MY DARN GUN!
CONTACT. TARGET CONFIRMED AS THE TERRORIST PRINCESS, LEIA ORGANA.
GAAGH!
THIS IS A PRINCESS?
SHUT UP AND TAKE HER DOWN!

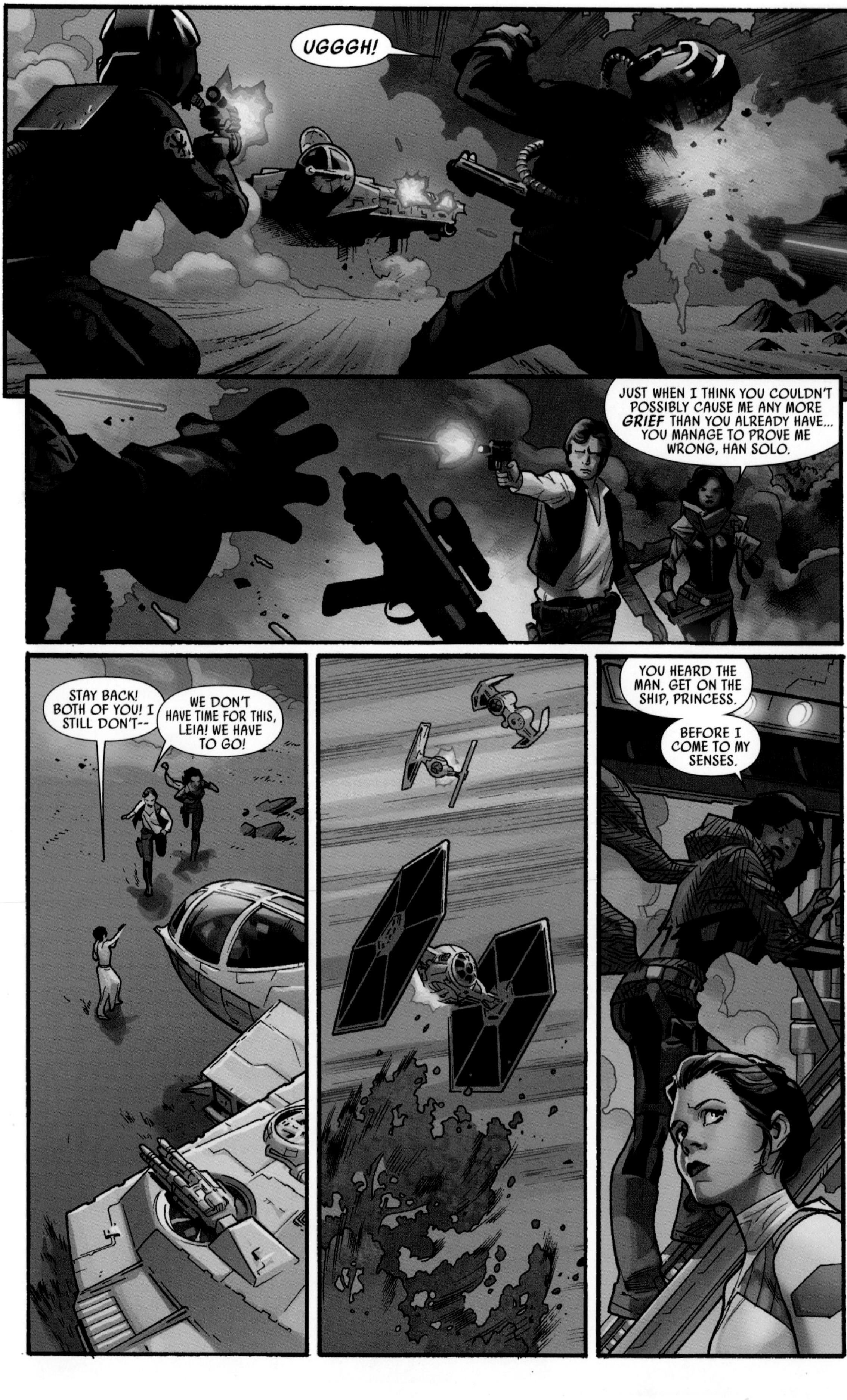
UGGGH!
JUST WHEN I THINK YOU COULDN'T POSSIBLY CAUSE ME ANY MORE GRIEF THAN YOU ALREADY HAVE... YOU MANAGE TO PROVE ME WRONG, HAN SOLO.
STAY BACK! BOTH OF YOU! I STILL DON'T--
WE DON'T HAVE TIME FOR THIS, LEIA! WE HAVE TO GO!
YOU HEARD THE MAN. GET ON THE SHIP, PRINCESS.
BEFORE I COME TO MY SENSES.

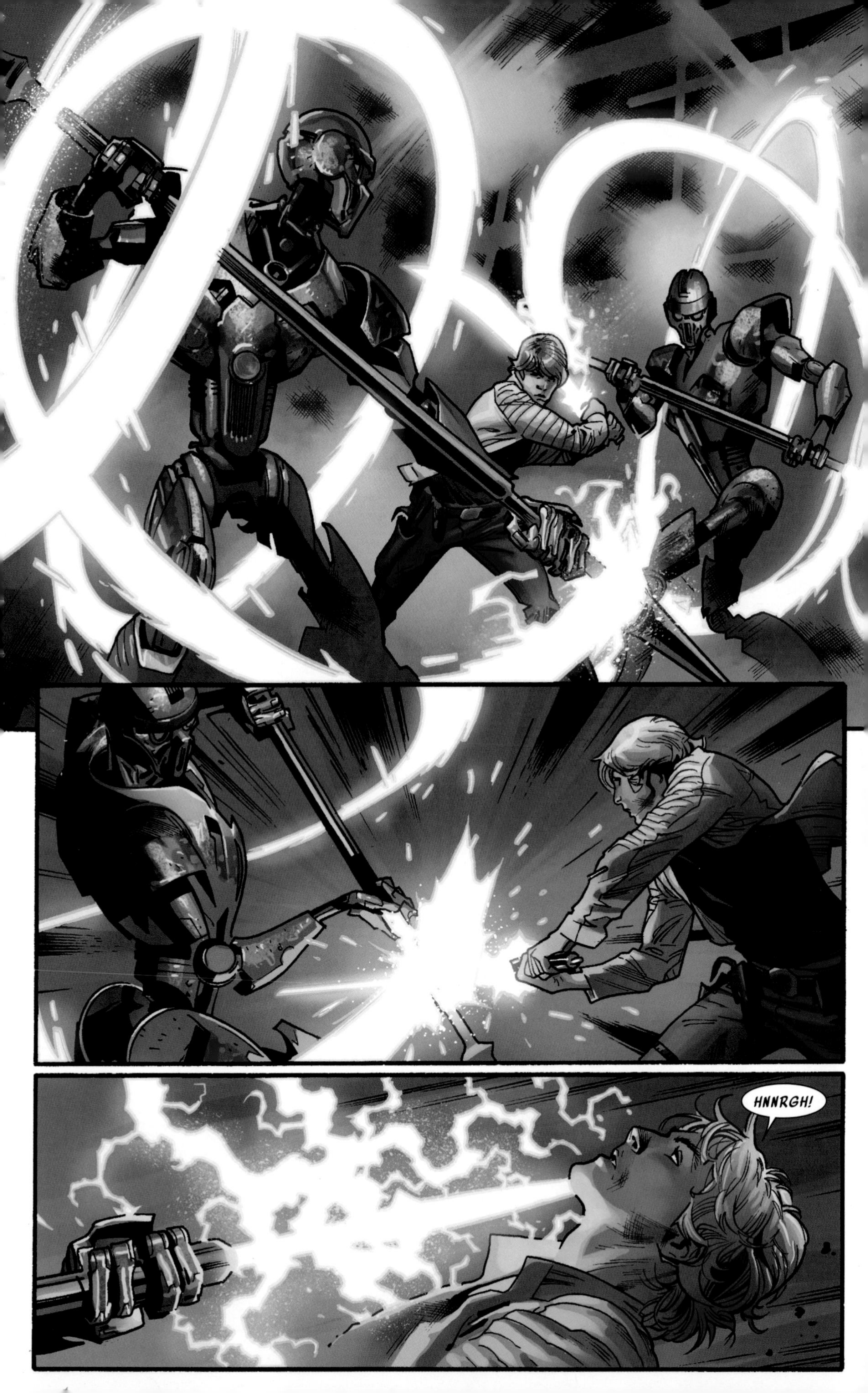
HNNRGH!

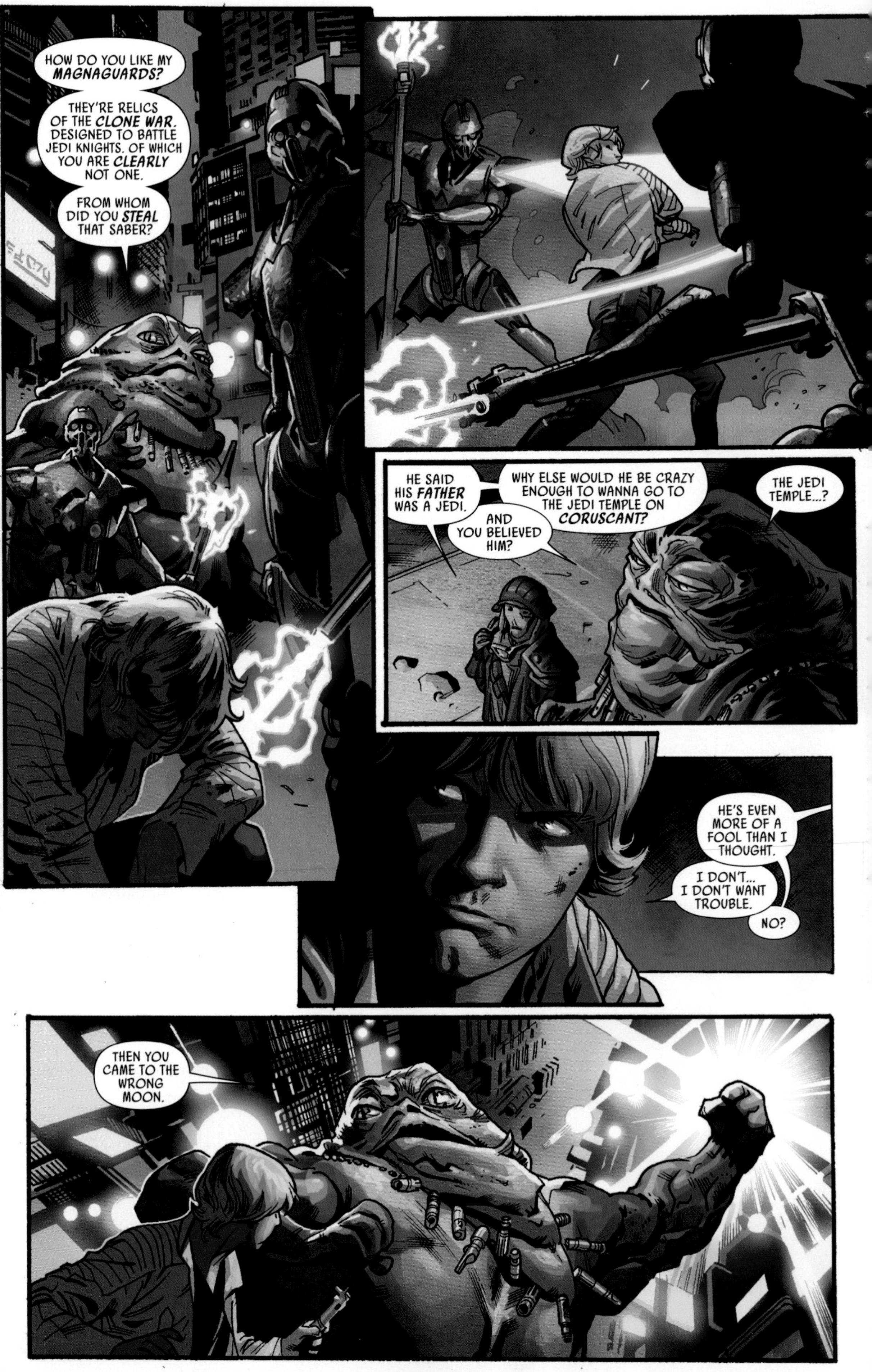
HOW DO YOU LIKE MY MAGNAGUARDS?
THEY'RE RELICS OF THE CLONE WAR. DESIGNED TO BATTLE JEDI KNIGHTS. OF WHICH YOU ARE CLEARLY NOT ONE.
FROM WHOM DID YOU STEAL THAT SABER?
HE SAID HIS FATHER WAS A JEDI.
WHY ELSE WOULD HE BE CRAZY ENOUGH TO WANNA GO TO THE JEDI TEMPLE ON CORUSCANT?
AND YOU BELIEVED HIM?
THE JEDI TEMPLE...?
HE'S EVEN MORE OF A FOOL THAN I THOUGHT.
I DON'T... I DON'T WANT TROUBLE.
NO?
THEN YOU CAME TO THE WRONG MOON.

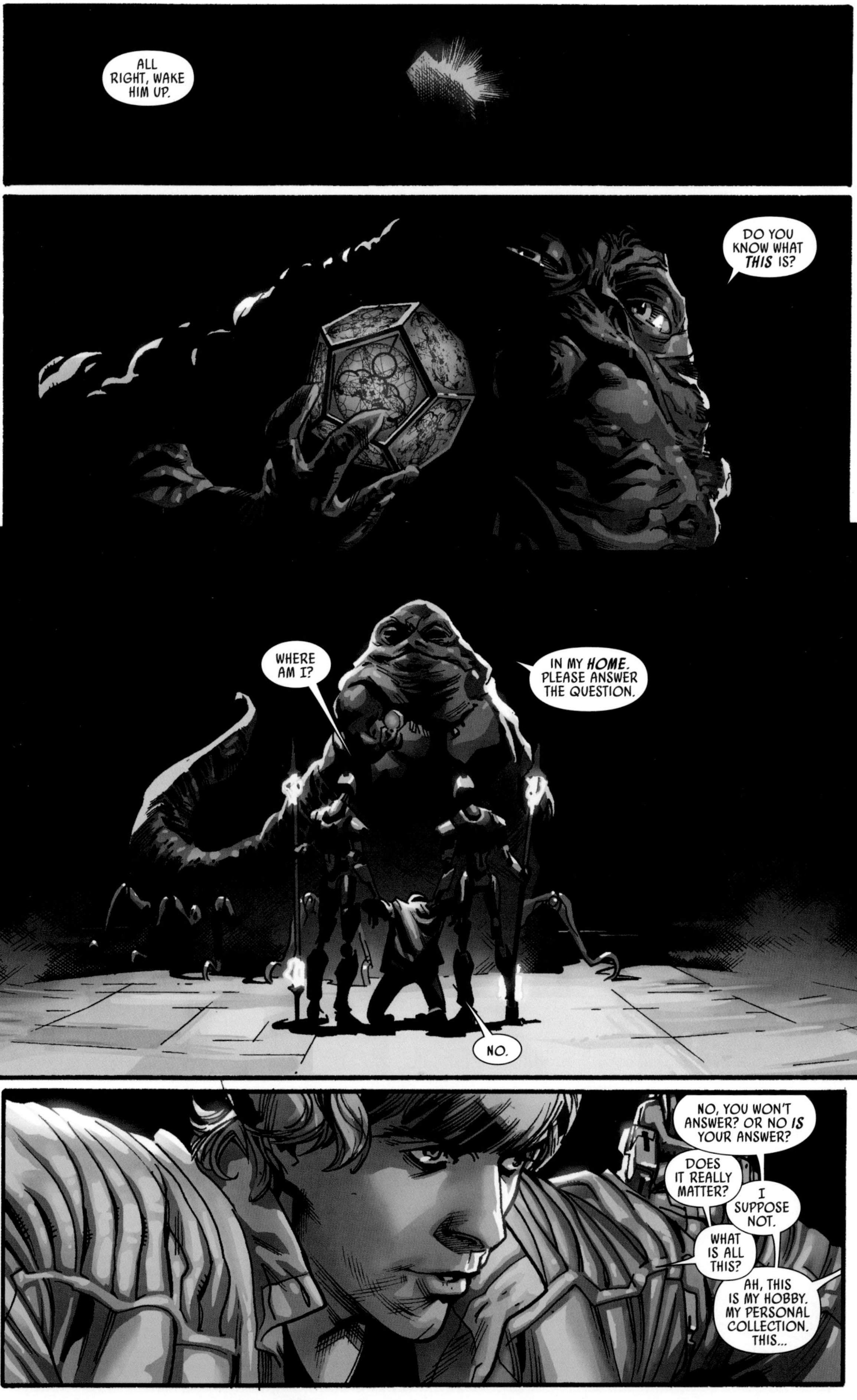
ALL RIGHT, WAKE HIM UP.
DO YOU KNOW WHAT *THIS* IS?
WHERE AM I?
IN MY *HOME*. PLEASE ANSWER THE QUESTION.
NO.
NO, YOU WON'T ANSWER? OR NO *IS* YOUR ANSWER?
DOES IT REALLY MATTER?
I SUPPOSE NOT.
WHAT IS ALL THIS?
AH, THIS IS MY HOBBY. MY PERSONAL COLLECTION. THIS...

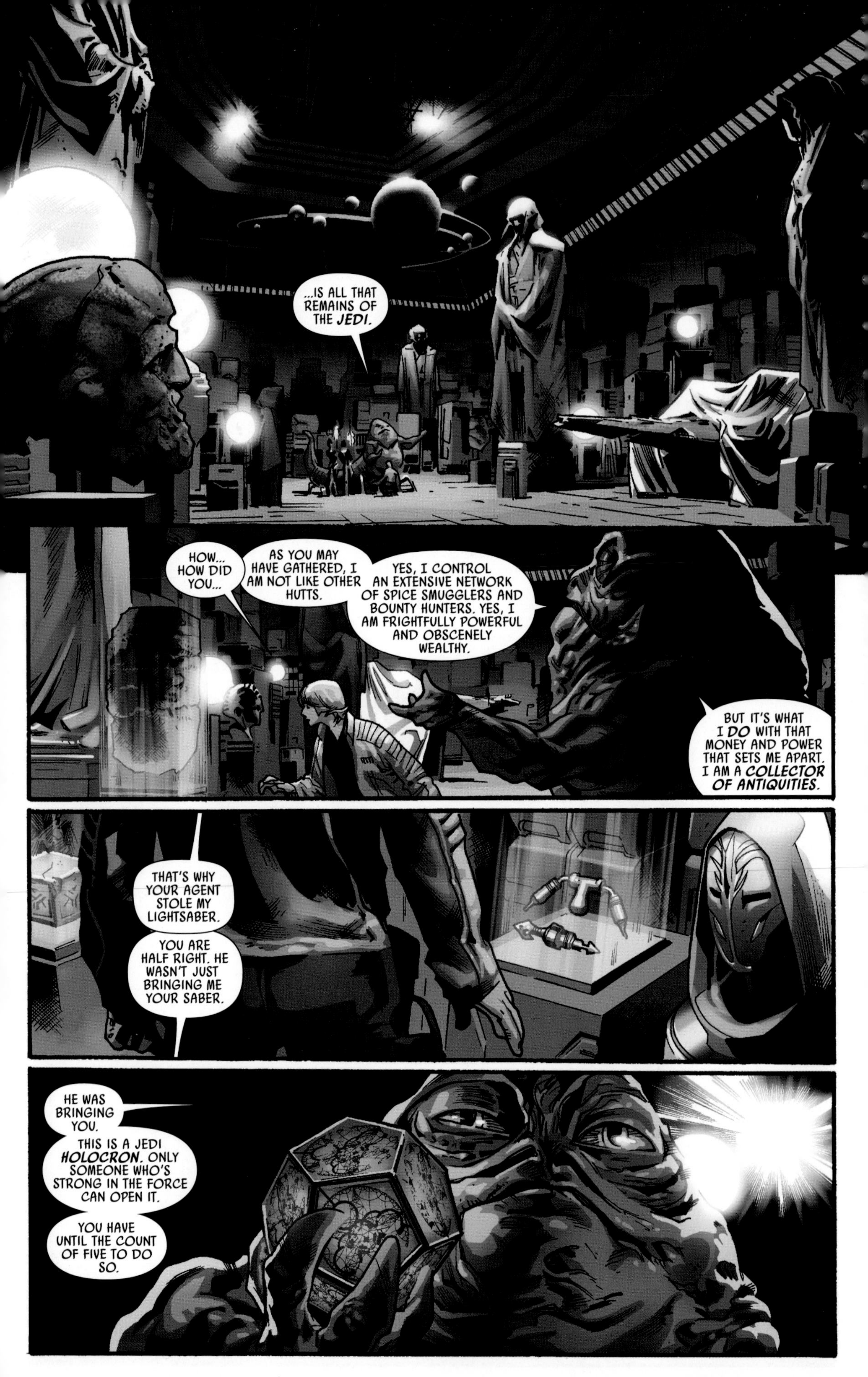
...IS ALL THAT REMAINS OF THE JEDI.
HOW... HOW DID YOU...
AS YOU MAY HAVE GATHERED, I AM NOT LIKE OTHER HUTTS.
YES, I CONTROL AN EXTENSIVE NETWORK OF SPICE SMUGGLERS AND BOUNTY HUNTERS. YES, I AM FRIGHTFULLY POWERFUL AND OBSCENELY WEALTHY.
BUT IT'S WHAT I DO WITH THAT MONEY AND POWER THAT SETS ME APART. I AM A COLLECTOR OF ANTIQUITIES.
THAT'S WHY YOUR AGENT STOLE MY LIGHTSABER.
YOU ARE HALF RIGHT. HE WASN'T JUST BRINGING ME YOUR SABER.
HE WAS BRINGING YOU.
THIS IS A JEDI HOLOCRON. ONLY SOMEONE WHO'S STRONG IN THE FORCE CAN OPEN IT.
YOU HAVE UNTIL THE COUNT OF FIVE TO DO SO.

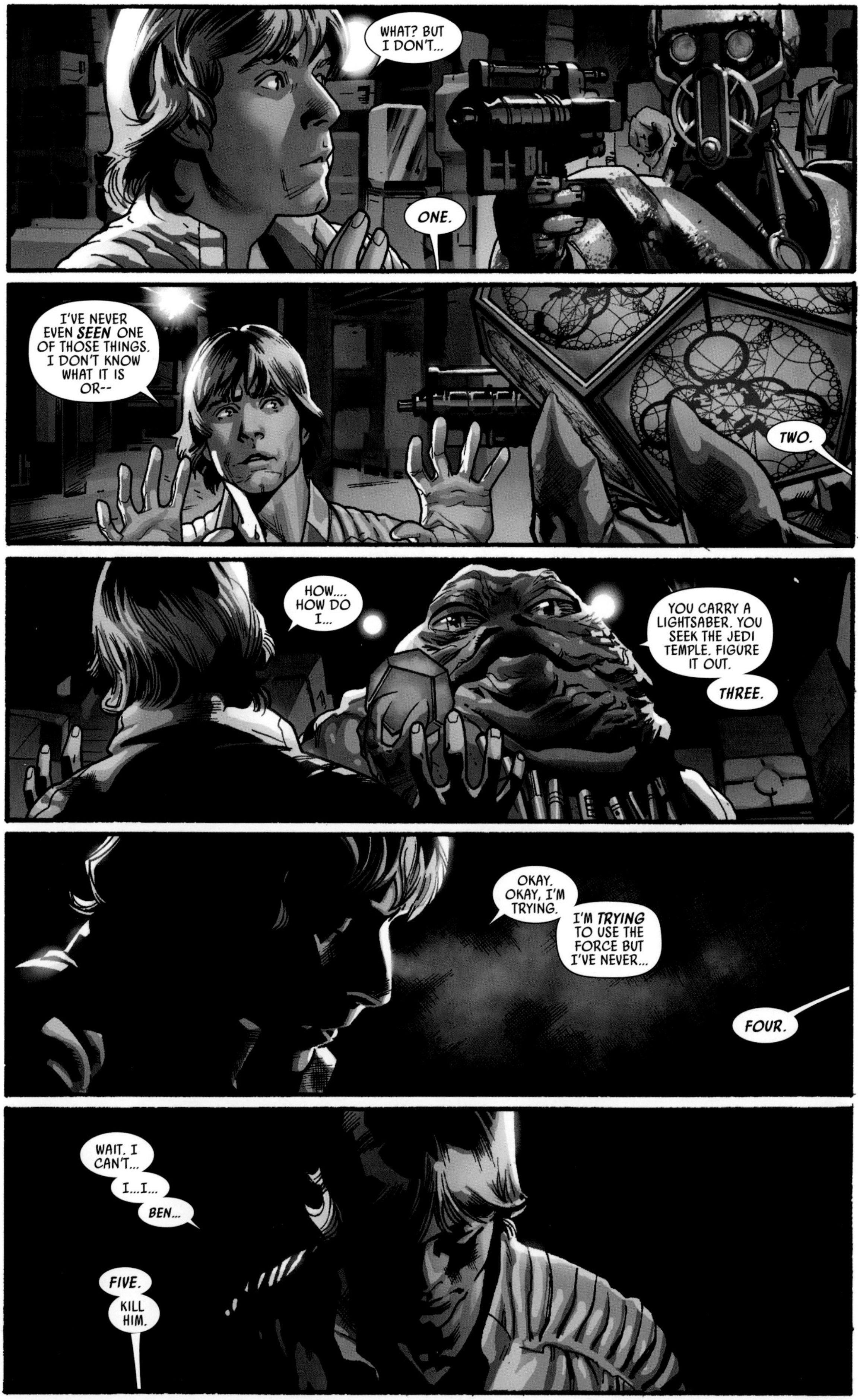

WHAT? BUT I DON'T...
ONE.
I'VE NEVER EVEN SEEN ONE OF THOSE THINGS. I DON'T KNOW WHAT IT IS OR--
TWO.
HOW.... HOW DO I...
YOU CARRY A LIGHTSABER. YOU SEEK THE JEDI TEMPLE. FIGURE IT OUT.
THREE.
OKAY. OKAY, I'M TRYING.
I'M TRYING TO USE THE FORCE BUT I'VE NEVER...
FOUR.
WAIT. I CAN'T...
I...I...
BEN...
FIVE.
KILL HIM.

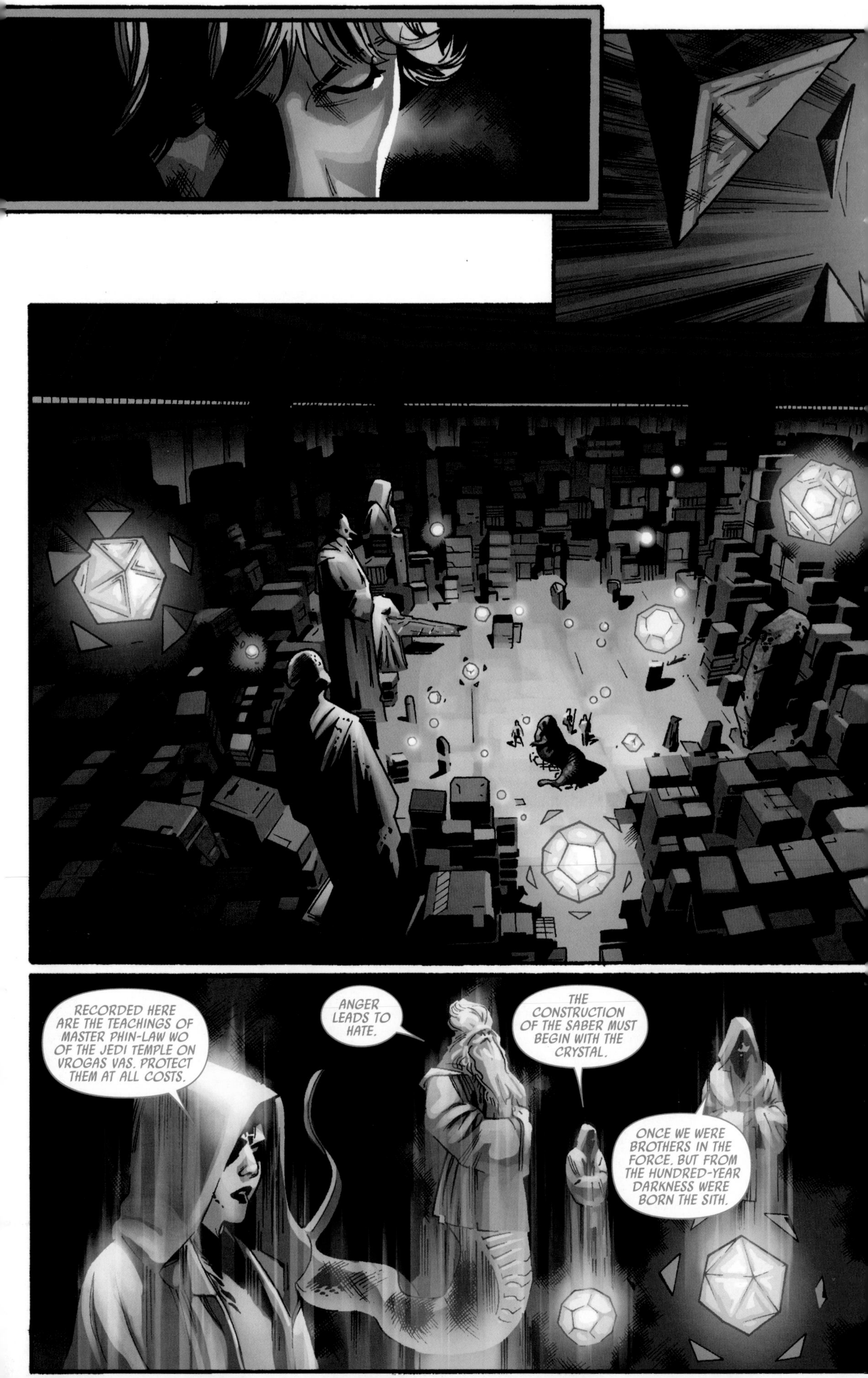
RECORDED HERE ARE THE TEACHINGS OF MASTER PHIN-LAW WO OF THE JEDI TEMPLE ON VROGAS VAS. PROTECT THEM AT ALL COSTS.
ANGER LEADS TO HATE.
THE CONSTRUCTION OF THE SABER MUST BEGIN WITH THE CRYSTAL.
ONCE WE WERE BROTHERS IN THE FORCE, BUT FROM THE HUNDRED-YEAR DARKNESS WERE BORN THE SITH.

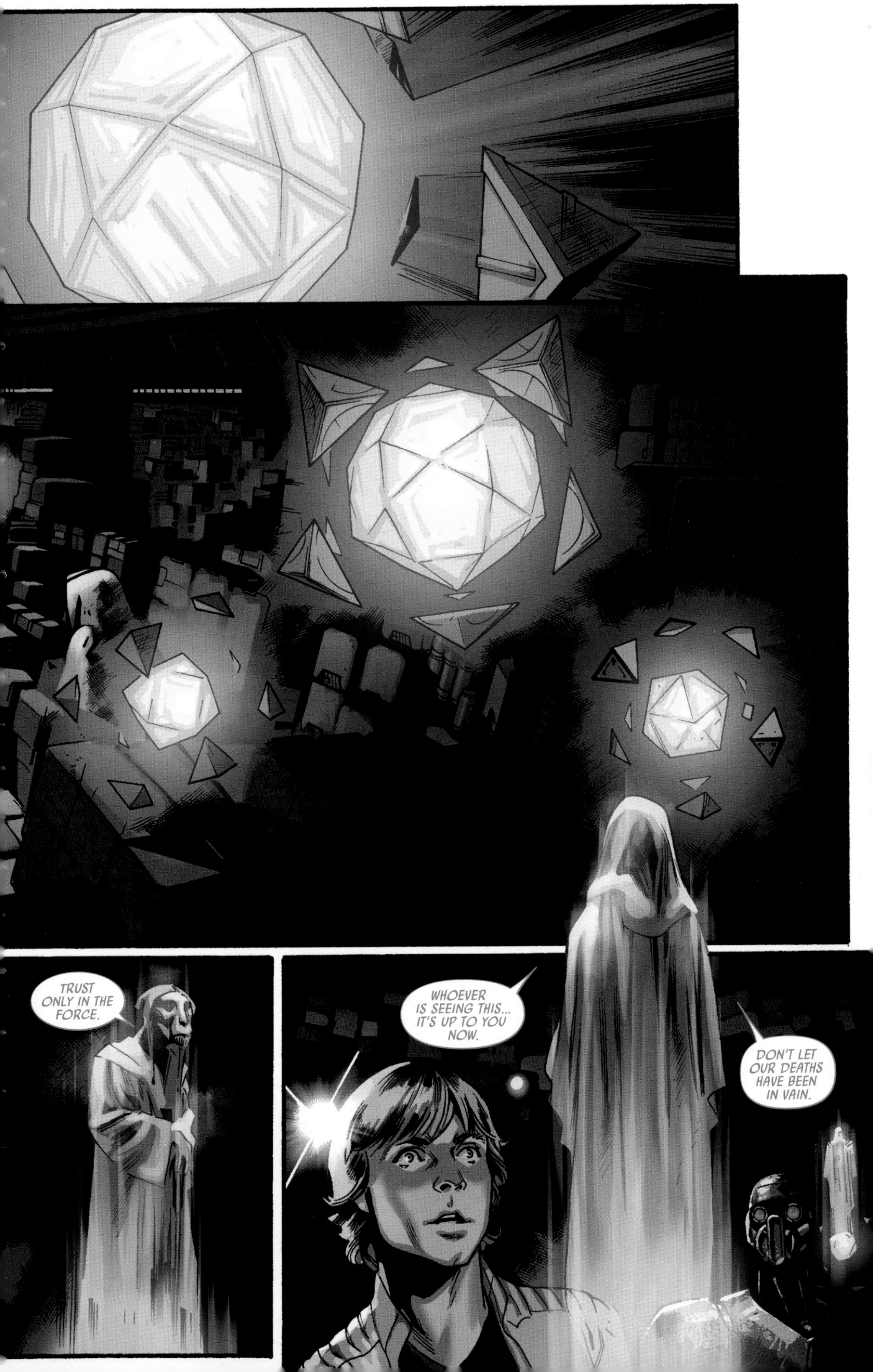
TRUST ONLY IN THE FORCE.
WHOEVER IS SEEING THIS... IT'S UP TO YOU NOW.
DON'T LET OUR DEATHS HAVE BEEN IN VAIN.

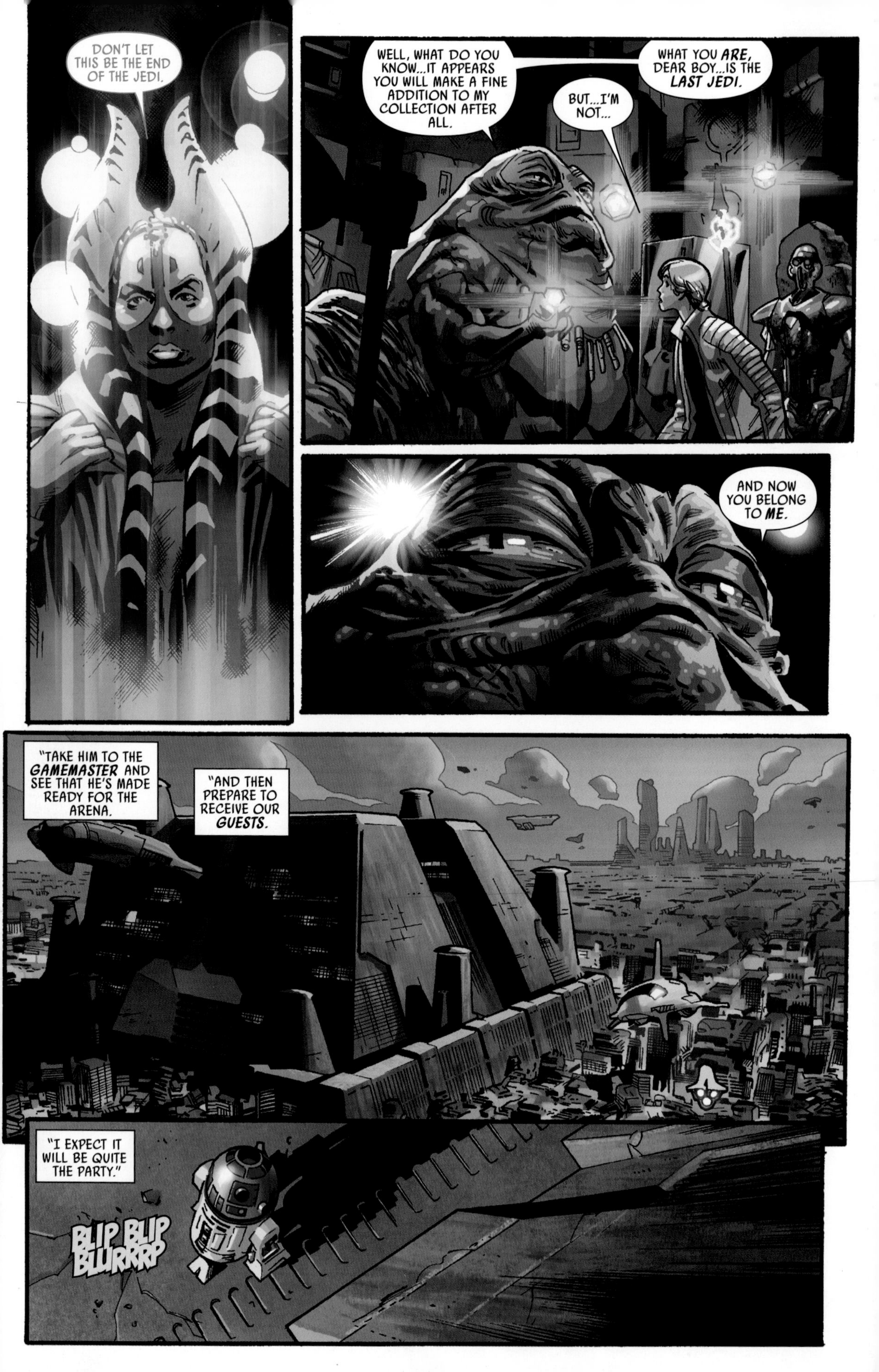
DON'T LET THIS BE THE END OF THE JEDI.
WELL, WHAT DO YOU KNOW...IT APPEARS YOU WILL MAKE A FINE ADDITION TO MY COLLECTION AFTER ALL.
BUT...I'M NOT...
WHAT YOU ARE, DEAR BOY...IS THE LAST JEDI.
AND NOW YOU BELONG TO ME.
"TAKE HIM TO THE GAMEMASTER AND SEE THAT HE'S MADE READY FOR THE ARENA.
"AND THEN PREPARE TO RECEIVE OUR GUESTS.
"I EXPECT IT WILL BE QUITE THE PARTY."
BLIP BLIP BLURRRP

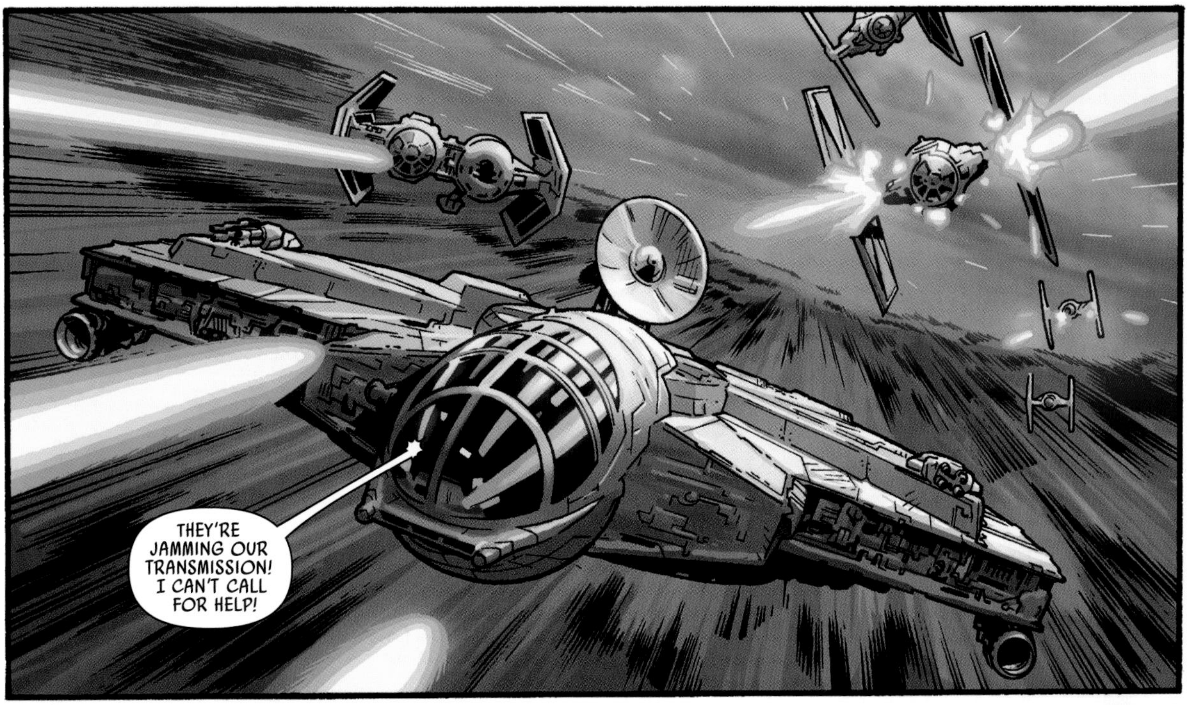
THEY'RE JAMMING OUR TRANSMISSION! I CAN'T CALL FOR HELP!

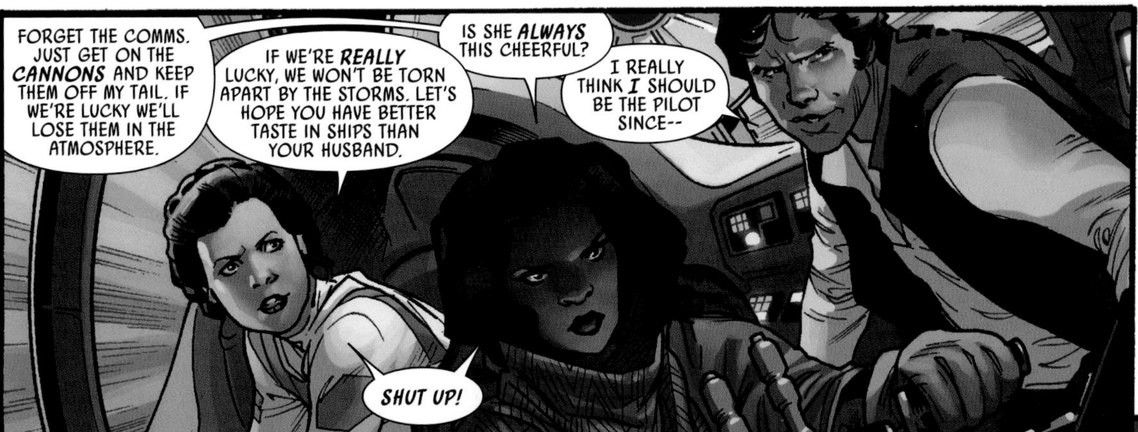
FORGET THE COMMS. JUST GET ON THE CANNONS AND KEEP THEM OFF MY TAIL. IF WE'RE LUCKY WE'LL LOSE THEM IN THE ATMOSPHERE.
IF WE'RE REALLY LUCKY, WE WON'T BE TORN APART BY THE STORMS. LET'S HOPE YOU HAVE BETTER TASTE IN SHIPS THAN YOUR HUSBAND.
IS SHE ALWAYS THIS CHEERFUL?
I REALLY THINK I SHOULD BE THE PILOT SINCE--
SHUT UP!

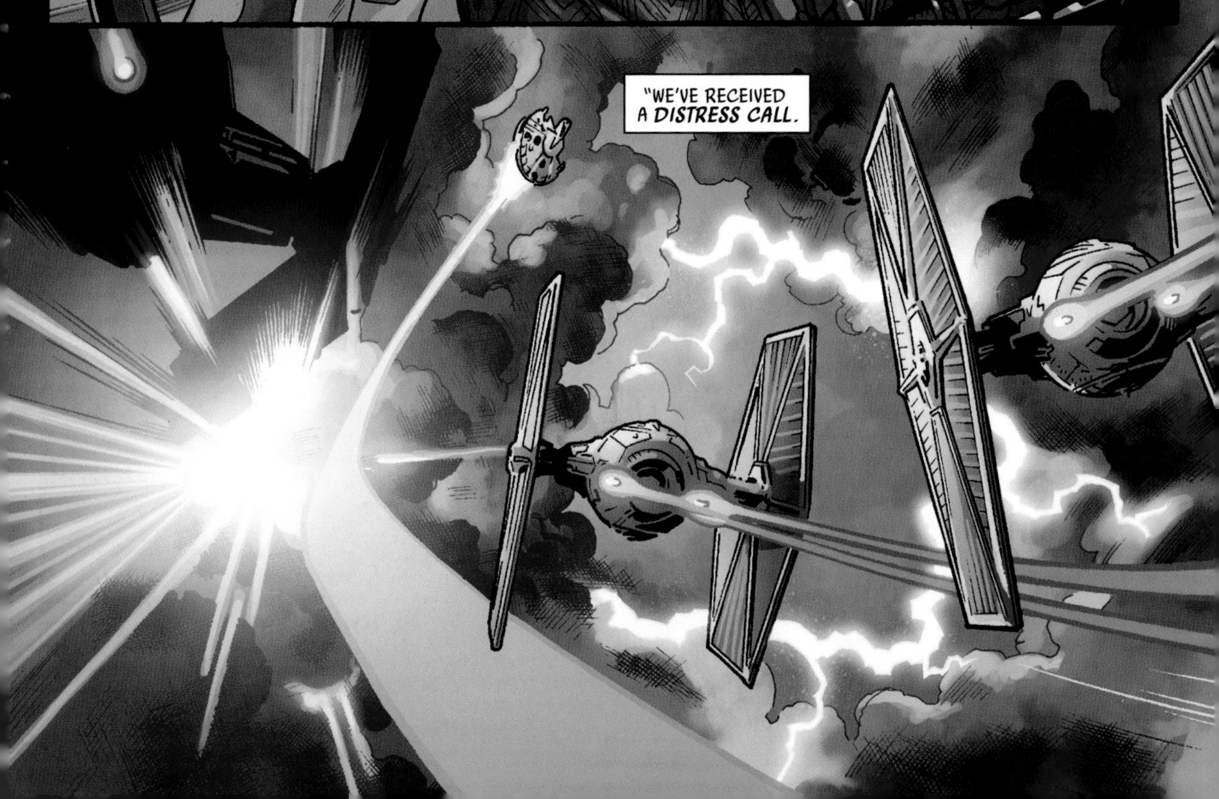
"WE'VE RECEIVED A DISTRESS CALL.

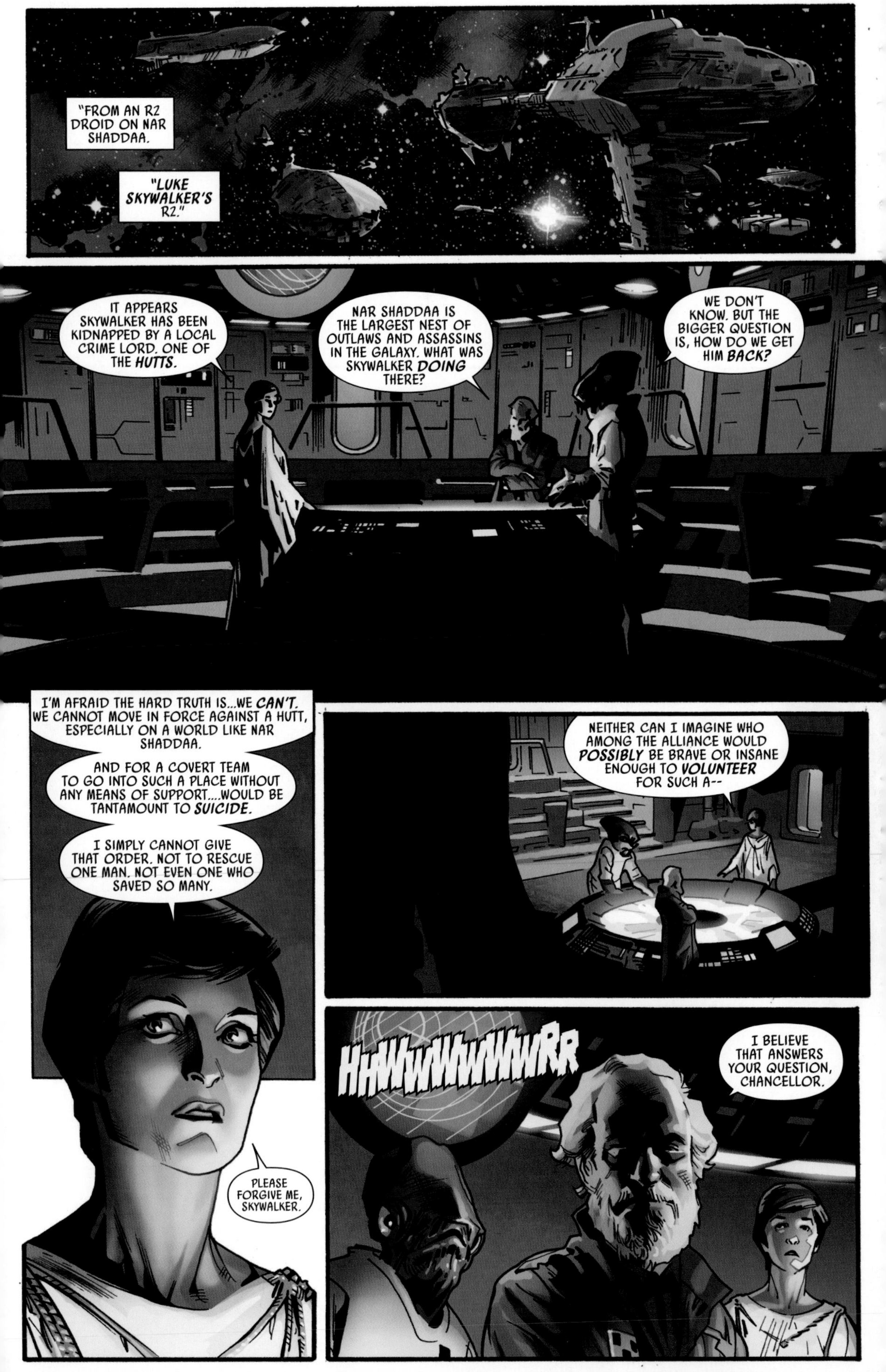
"FROM AN R2 DROID ON NAR SHADDAA.
"LUKE SKYWALKER'S R2."
IT APPEARS SKYWALKER HAS BEEN KIDNAPPED BY A LOCAL CRIME LORD. ONE OF THE HUTTS.
NAR SHADDAA IS THE LARGEST NEST OF OUTLAWS AND ASSASSINS IN THE GALAXY. WHAT WAS SKYWALKER DOING THERE?
WE DON'T KNOW. BUT THE BIGGER QUESTION IS, HOW DO WE GET HIM BACK?
I'M AFRAID THE HARD TRUTH IS...WE CAN'T. WE CANNOT MOVE IN FORCE AGAINST A HUTT, ESPECIALLY ON A WORLD LIKE NAR SHADDAA.
AND FOR A COVERT TEAM TO GO INTO SUCH A PLACE WITHOUT ANY MEANS OF SUPPORT....WOULD BE TANTAMOUNT TO SUICIDE.
I SIMPLY CANNOT GIVE THAT ORDER. NOT TO RESCUE ONE MAN. NOT EVEN ONE WHO SAVED SO MANY.
PLEASE FORGIVE ME, SKYWALKER.
NEITHER CAN I IMAGINE WHO AMONG THE ALLIANCE WOULD POSSIBLY BE BRAVE OR INSANE ENOUGH TO VOLUNTEER FOR SUCH A--
HHWWWWWWWRR
I BELIEVE THAT ANSWERS YOUR QUESTION, CHANCELLOR.

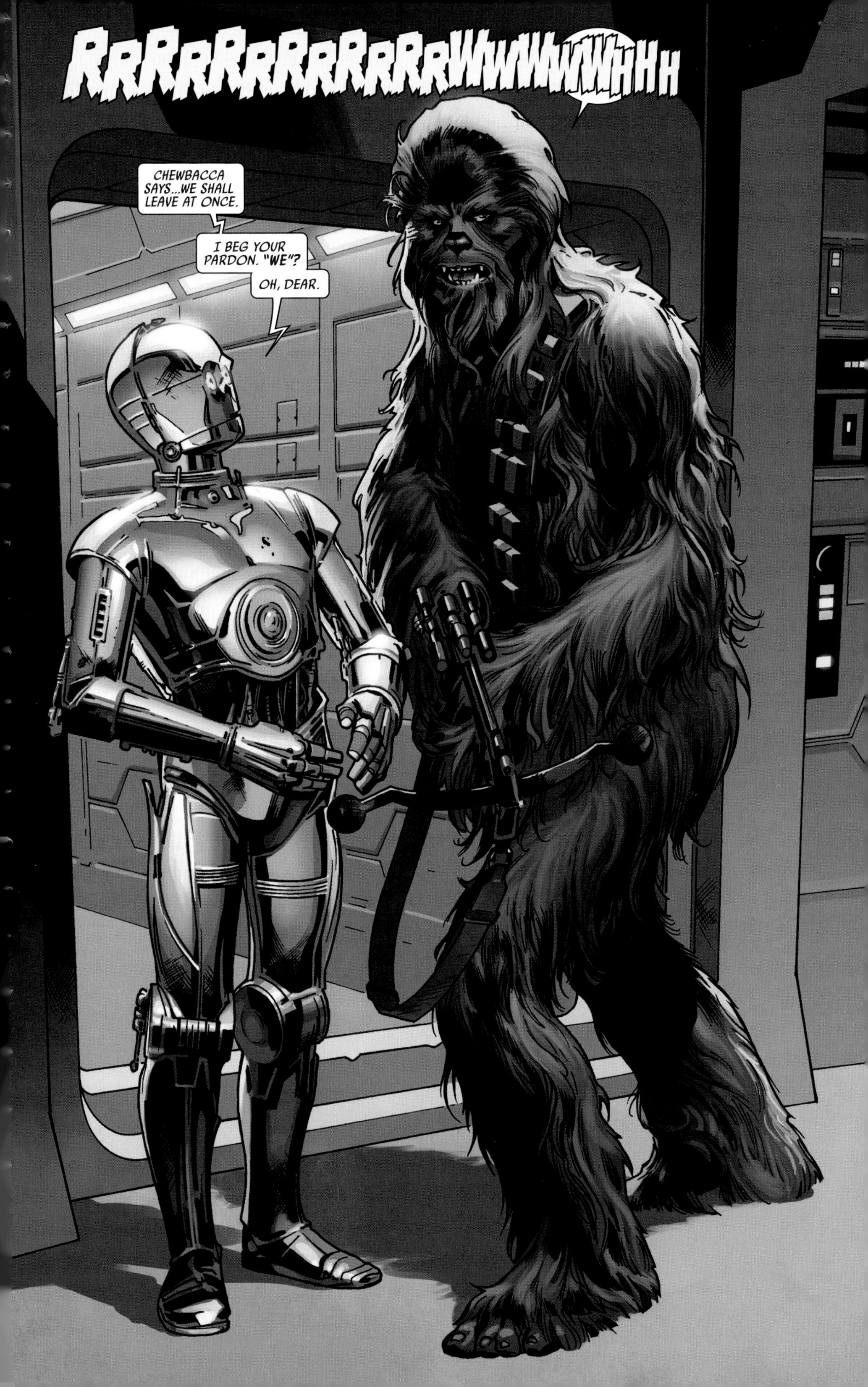
RRRRRRRRRRRRRRRWWWWWWWHHH
CHEWBACCA SAYS...WE SHALL LEAVE AT ONCE.
I BEG YOUR PARDON. "WE"?
OH, DEAR.

STAR WARS

SHOWDOWN ON THE SMUGGLER'S MOON

COLLECT THEM ALL!

Set of 6 Hardcover Books ISBN: 978-1-61479-553-7

STAR WARS
STAR WARS
SHOWDOWN ON THE SMUGGLER'S MOON: VOLUME 1
AARON BIANCHI PONSOR

Hardcover Book ISBN
978-1-61479-554-4

STAR WARS
STAR WARS
SHOWDOWN ON THE SMUGGLER'S MOON: VOLUME 2
AARON IMMONEN VON GRAWBADGER PONSOR

Hardcover Book ISBN
978-1-61479-555-1

STAR WARS
STAR WARS
SHOWDOWN ON THE SMUGGLER'S MOON: VOLUME 3
AARON IMMONEN VON GRAWBADGER PONSOR

Hardcover Book ISBN
978-1-61479-556-8

STAR WARS
STAR WARS
SHOWDOWN ON THE SMUGGLER'S MOON: VOLUME 4
AARON IMMONEN VON GRAWBADGER PONSOR

Hardcover Book ISBN
978-1-61479-557-5

STAR WARS
STAR WARS
SHOWDOWN ON THE SMUGGLER'S MOON: VOLUME 5
AARON IMMONEN VON GRAWBADGER PONSOR

Hardcover Book ISBN
978-1-61479-558-2

STAR WARS
STAR WARS
SHOWDOWN ON THE SMUGGLER'S MOON: VOLUME 6
AARON IMMONEN VON GRAWBADGER PONSOR

Hardcover Book ISBN
978-1-61479-559-9

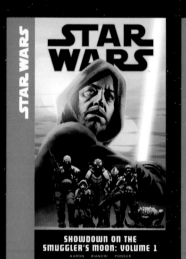

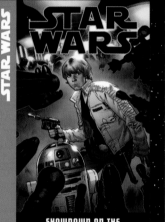

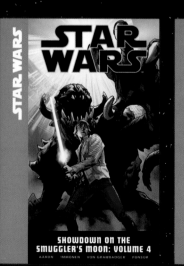

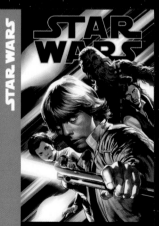